John C. Haines School
247 W. 23rd Place
Chicago, IL 60616
Diann Wright, Principal

Young Cam Jansen

and the
Library Mystery

BY **DAVID A. ADLER**

ILLUSTRATED BY **SUSANNA NATTI**

PUFFIN BOOKS

Best wishes for happy reading always to
Sophia Judith Brodie-Weisberg
—D. A. and S.N.

PUFFIN BOOKS
Published by the Penguin Group
Penguin Putnam Books for Young Readers, 345 Hudson Street, New York, New York 10014, U.S.A.
Penguin Books Ltd, 80 Strand, London WC2R ORL, England
Penguin Books Australia Ltd, Ringwood, Victoria, Australia
Penguin Books Canada Ltd, 10 Alcorn Avenue, Toronto, Ontario, Canada M4V 3B2
Penguin Books (N.Z.) Ltd, 182-190 Wairau Road, Auckland 10, New Zealand

Penguin Books Ltd, Registered Offices: Harmondsworth, Middlesex, England

First published in the United States of America by Viking,
a division of Penguin Putnam Books for Young Readers, 2001
Published by Puffin Books, a division of Penguin Putnam Books for Young Readers, 2002

1 3 5 7 9 10 8 6 4 2

THE LIBRARY OF CONGRESS HAS CATALOGED THE VIKING EDITION AS FOLLOWS:
Adler, David A.
Young Cam Jansen and the library mystery/ by David A. Adler ; illustrated by Susanna Natti.
p.   cm. – [A Viking easy-to-read. Level 2]
Summary: Cam uses her photographic memory to find a shopping list that her dad lost at the library.
ISBN 0-670-89281-5 (hc)
[1. Memory—Fiction. 2. Mystery and detective stories.]
I. Natti, Susanna, ill. II. Title. III. Series.
PZ7.A2615 Yor 2001 [Fic]—dc21   00-010969

Puffin Books ISBN 0-14-230202-3
Printed in Hong Kong
Set in Bookman

Reading Level 2.0

CONTENTS

Cam Jansen has an amazing memory. Do you?

Look at this picture. Blink your eyes and say "Click!" Then turn to the last page of this book.

1. BLUEBERRIES ON THE LOOSE!

"Look at all these mysteries,"

Cam Jansen said.

"I love mysteries."

Cam was in the library with her father

and her friend Eric Shelton.

"I'm borrowing this book," Cam said.

"It's a dinosaur mystery."

"And I'm borrowing this one," Eric said.

"It's about a boy

who gets into lots of trouble."

5

Their friend Jason was in the library, too.

Jason showed Cam and Eric a book.

"Does this look good?" he asked.

"That's *Blueberries on the Loose!*" Cam said.

"It's one of my favorite books."

Cam closed her eyes and said, "Click."

"The story begins in a supermarket," Cam said.

Jason opened the book.

"Little Eddie looked at the tower of boxes,"

Cam said with her eyes still closed.

"'Blueberries,' Little Eddie said.

He took a box and the whole tower fell.

'Blueberries on the loose!'

Little Eddie said."

"Wow!" Jason told Cam.

"That's exactly what's printed here."

Cam has an amazing memory.

She says her memory is like a camera.

She says she has a picture in her head

of everything she's seen.

Cam says Click is the sound her camera makes.

"There's a great picture on the first page,"

Cam told Jason.

"There are blueberries everywhere.

There are even two in Little Eddie's hair."

Cam's real name is Jennifer.

But because of her great memory

people started calling her "the Camera."

Then "the Camera" became just Cam.

"We have to go," Eric told Cam.

"Your father is in a hurry.

After we leave the library,

we're going to the supermarket."

Jason laughed.

"Be careful in the supermarket," he said.

"Don't have a blueberry accident."

2. WATCH OUT!

Mr. Jansen was sitting

near the front of the library.

He was reading a mystery.

"We're ready," Cam told him.

Mr. Jansen looked up.

"This is a great book.

I'm already on page 10."

Mr. Jansen put in a bookmark

and closed the book.

He walked with Cam and Eric

to the check-out desk.

A line of people waited there

to borrow books.

Cam closed her eyes.

She said, "Click."

Then she told Eric,

"Little Eddie's father

helped clean up the blueberries.

Little Eddie reached for a tower of peaches."

"Oh, no!" Eric said.

Cam told Eric, "Little Eddie's father was quick.

He pulled Eddie away just in time."

"That was good," Eric said.

"No it wasn't," Cam said.

"He pulled Eddie into a tower

of canned tomatoes."

"Oh, no," Eric said.

"Oh, yes," Cam told him.

"Cans rolled all over the store."

"Let's go," Mr. Jansen told Cam and Eric.

"Our books are checked out."

When they got to the supermarket,

Cam took a shopping cart.

She followed her father and Eric.

There were magazines and books for sale

just inside the supermarket.

There were towers of tissue boxes,

canned peaches, and blueberries.

"Watch out!" Eric told Cam.

"We don't want a blueberry accident."

13

As they walked into the store

Cam asked her father,

"What are we buying?"

Mr. Jansen reached into his shirt pocket.

He reached into his other pockets, too.

Then he shook his head and said,

"I don't know what we need to buy.

I lost the shopping list."

3. THAT'S WHERE I WAS

Eric said, "Maybe Cam remembers

what is on the list."

Cam shook her head and said,

"No. I never really looked at it."

"I know I had it this morning,"

Mr. Jansen said.

"I remember putting it in my shirt pocket."

"We need lettuce and tomatoes," Cam said.

"We need peppers, cucumbers, carrots, and

onions. Mom wants to make a salad."

15

"There was a lot more on the list,"

Mr. Jansen said.

"It was a very long list.

I looked at it when I was in the library."

Mr. Jansen checked his pockets again.

He took out some coins, keys, and his wallet.

Eric said, "Maybe it's *in* your wallet."

Mr. Jansen looked in his wallet.

He didn't find the list.

Mr. Jansen turned.

He pointed to the front of the store.

"That's where I was

when I first looked for the list.

Maybe it fell out of my pocket."

A worker was sweeping

the front of the store.

17

Eric ran to him.

"Did you find a long piece of paper?" Eric

asked. "It's our shopping list."

"I found lots of papers," the man said.

"That's why I'm sweeping."

"Did you find one right now

and right here?" Mr. Jansen asked.

The man stopped sweeping.

He rubbed his chin and said,

"I really don't know.

I don't look at what I sweep up.

I just sweep everything into that corner.

Later, I put it all in the trash bin."

"It must be over there," Eric said.

He pointed to the corner.

"That's where we'll find the shopping list."

4. CAM SAID, "CLICK!"

Cam, Eric, and Mr. Jansen

hurried to the corner of the store.

"Here's a shopping list," Eric said.

He took the paper off the floor.

"Eggs, corn oil, sardines,"

Eric read from the list.

"That's not ours," Mr. Jansen said.

"We don't eat sardines."

Cam looked at the list.

"Someone threw this out," Cam said.

"There's a check next to everything."

There were other papers on the floor,

but no other shopping lists.

"Maybe I dropped it in the car,"

Mr. Jansen said.

"Maybe I dropped it in the library."

Mr. Jansen turned.

He walked toward the exit.

Cam and Eric followed him.

Cam looked at the magazines and books.

She looked at the towers of tissue boxes,

canned peaches, and blueberries.

Cam looked at the books again.

Lots of them were mysteries.

"Oh," Cam said, and closed her eyes.

Cam said, "Click!"

She quickly opened her eyes.

"Wait!" she told her father and Eric.

Eric and Mr. Jansen stopped by the exit.

Cam closed her eyes.

She said, "Click!" again.

"Oh," she said with her eyes still closed. "There it is. I'm looking at a picture of a small piece of the shopping list. I'm looking at it right now!"

5. LET'S GO SHOPPING

"Just a small piece?" Eric asked.

"Look at the whole list

and tell your father what to buy."

"Please, excuse me," a woman said.

She was pushing a shopping cart.

She was trying to leave the supermarket.

Eric and Mr. Jansen moved out of her way.

"I can't see the whole list," Cam said.

"I can only see the very top of it."

"Excuse me," a man said.

He was pushing a cart, too.

"We can't stand here," Mr. Jansen told Cam.

"Open your eyes and come outside."

Cam opened her eyes.

She pushed their cart out of the store.

Eric asked, "Is the list in the library?"

"Well," Cam said and smiled.

"It is and it isn't."

"Let's go," Mr. Jansen said. "It's late.

We have to get back to the library

and get that list."

"No we don't," Cam said.

"We don't?" Eric asked.

"Just go to the car," Cam said.

"The mystery you borrowed

is on the front seat.

Open it to page 10

and you'll find the shopping list."

Cam, Eric, and Mr. Jansen went to the car.

"How do you know it's there?" Eric asked.

Cam told Eric, "Dad said

he had the list in the library.

So I looked at the pictures

I had in my head.

Dad was sitting in the library.

He was holding a book

and a piece of paper."

"Yes," Eric said. "I saw that, too."

Cam said, "That piece of paper

must have been the list.

When he got up to check out our books,

he was not holding the paper.

So he must have used it as a bookmark."

Mr. Jansen opened the car door.

Eric said, "And that's why you saw

just the top of the list.

You looked at the picture

you have in your head of your father's book.

Just the top of the list was sticking out."

"Here it is," Mr. Jansen told Cam.

"It was just where you said it would be."

They walked toward the store again.

Mr. Jansen said, "I love reading mysteries,

but I'm not good at solving them."

"Cam is really good at solving mysteries,"

Eric said.

"Yes she is," Mr. Jansen said proudly.

Cam, Eric, and Mr. Jansen

walked into the supermarket again.

Mr. Jansen looked at the list.

Then he showed it to Cam.

"Please, look at this, too," he said.

Cam looked at the list.

She blinked her eyes and said, "Click."

"Good," Mr. Jansen said.

"Now even if I lose the list

we have an extra copy of it."

"Yes," Cam said.

She pointed to her head.

"I have a picture of it right here."

"Good," Mr. Jansen said again.

"Now let's do some shopping."

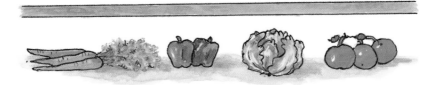

A Cam Jansen
Memory Game

Take another look at the picture on page 4.

Study it.

Blink your eyes and say, "Click!"

Then turn back to this page

and answer these questions:

1. Is Cam wearing a skirt, pants, or shorts?

2. Where are the flowers?

3. How many people are in the picture, 6, 8, 10, or 12?

4. What is on the table, new books, old books, or sale books?

5. Is the book Cam is holding open or closed?